# The Sea Dog

## Written by Penny Matthews
## Illustrated by Andrew McLean

An easy-to-read SOLO
for beginning readers

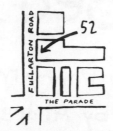

Omnibus Books
A.C.N. 000 614 577
52 Fullarton Road, Norwood, South Australia 5067
part of the SCHOLASTIC GROUP
Sydney · Auckland · New York · Toronto · London
www.scholastic.com.au

First published 1998
Reprinted 1998, 1999, 2000

Cover design by Lyn Mitchell
Typeset by Clinton Ellicott, MoBros, Adelaide
Printed and bound by Hyde Park Press, Adelaide

National Library of Australia Cataloguing-in-Publication entry
Matthews, P.E. (Penelope E.), 1945–   .
The sea dog.
ISBN 1 86291 375 7.
I. McLean, Andrew, 1946–   . II. Title. (Series:
(Solos (Norwood, S. Aust.)).

A823.3

*For Alison – P.M.*

*For Jackson and Gulliver – A.McL.*

## Chapter 1

Ben's home was a lighthouse. He lived there with his mum and his dad.

Ben liked living in a lighthouse, but it was a bit lonely.

No one lived near by, and there was no school. Ben did lessons every day with his mum.

Ben's bedroom had two windows.
From one of them he could see dark
scrub, and the thin dusty track that
led to the town, far away.

From the other he could see steep cliffs and sharp grey rocks. But most of all he could see the sea.

## Chapter 2

The sea never stopped moving. Even on sunny days waves smashed on the rocks. Spray shot up into the air like mist.

On bad days the wind howled around the lighthouse. The sea turned from blue to grey, and the waves had white caps.

Ben knew what could happen to ships at sea. He'd seen bits of broken ships washed up on the sharp rocks.

He knew how strong the sea was. He was afraid of the sea.

## Chapter 3

Every day, at sunset, Ben's dad turned on the big light at the top of the lighthouse.

The light told ships out at sea that there were rocks near by. *Danger*, it said. *Don't sail too close.*

The light sent out a long flash, and then two short ones. Over and over.

FLASH ... *flash flash* ... FLASH ... *flash flash*.

Ships, take care, said the light. Ships, take care.

Every night, before he fell asleep,
Ben hoped the ships would be safe.

But in his dreams the sea was
cold and grey, and very, very scary.

## Chapter 4

A little way from the lighthouse was a small bay. The rocks were round here, and the sea was gentle. The waves ran quickly up the sand and back again, leaving white foam.

Ben walked on the beach.

He made sand castles.

He did cartwheels,

and looked for shells.

But he never went near the water.
He didn't even want to paddle.

"One day I'll teach you to swim,
Ben," his mum said.

"No," said Ben.

## Chapter 5

Once a week Dad drove down the thin dusty track into the town.

He came home with meat and butter, flour and sugar. Often he had apples for Ben, or a bag of sweets.

One day he had a big surprise.

In the back of the truck was a
little white dog.

"She needs a friend," Dad told
Ben.

Ben lifted the little dog out of the truck. She licked him on the nose.

"I'll call you Licky," Ben told her.

## Chapter 6

Licky had a curly white coat like sea foam. Her nose was like a flat pink shell. Her eyes were shiny brown, the colour of wet seaweed.

"She's a sea dog," said Ben.

Licky went on walks with Ben,
through the scrub ...

... along the beach

... up and down the rocks.

She raced him up the stairs to his bedroom.

And every night, while the big light above them went FLASH … *flash flash* … FLASH … *flash flash*, she slept on the end of Ben's bed.

She was Ben's best friend.

## Chapter 7

One hot day Ben and Licky had a picnic on the beach.

Ben ate cake and apples and drank lemon drink. Licky ran after sea gulls and sniffed at jellyfish.

"Don't go in the water, Licky," said Ben. "It's not safe. Stay with me."

Licky stayed with Ben for a while, but she was hot.

She chased a sea gull into the
sea. The water was lovely and cool.

She ran through the waves.
*Splash, splash!*

Ben looked up.

Licky was in the water. All he could see was her little bobbing white head!

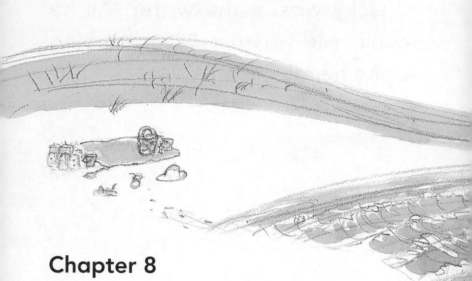

## Chapter 8

"Licky!" called Ben. "Licky! Come back!"

Ben knew how strong the sea was, but he had to help Licky. How could he stay on the beach and let her drown? She was his best friend.

He ran into the waves.

The water was cold around his feet.

Then it was up to his knees.

Up to his waist.

How cold it was! And how deep!

"Licky!" Ben shouted again.

A big wave pushed him over. Salt water filled his mouth.

Ben tried to get up, but another wave pushed him down again. Then —

Licky's little white head was bobbing close to Ben.

He held on to her neck. Her paws paddled strongly through the water.

Soon Ben's feet were on sand again.

The sun was hot, but Ben was cold. His legs felt weak.

Licky ran back into the sea and swam in a circle.

"Licky!" said Ben. "You can swim!"

Licky came out of the water and shook herself all over him. *Shake, shake, shake!*

Then she licked him on the nose.

## Chapter 9

"When I saw Licky in the water, I forgot I was afraid of the sea," Ben told Mum.

Mum hugged him. "It's lucky one of you knew how to swim," she said.

"I thought Licky would drown," said Ben. "But she's a real sea dog, isn't she?"

"All dogs can swim," said Mum. "Dogs love to swim."

"I'd like to swim like Licky," said Ben.

## Chapter 10

Mum showed Ben how to do the dog paddle, just like Licky.

Every day Ben and Licky played on the beach. They paddled and looked for crabs in the rock pools.

When it was hot, they went swimming. Sometimes Mum went swimming with them. Sometimes she sat on the sand and watched.

Soon Ben could swim just a little bit faster than Licky.

## Chapter 11

One hot night Ben couldn't sleep. He got out of bed and stood at his bedroom window.

He saw the lighthouse light shining in the darkness. FLASH ... *flash flash* ... FLASH ... *flash flash*. Keeping the ships safe.

Ben knew how strong the sea could be.

Like the ships, he would always take care.

He went back to bed, and Licky curled up at his feet.

That night Ben dreamed about the sea. But in his dream the sea wasn't cold and grey and scary. It was bright blue.

**Penny Matthews**

I love the sea. I love its colours, and its fresh salty smell, and the way it moves and changes all the time. But I'm a little bit scared of it. It's so BIG! I never learned to swim properly, so for me one of the best things about the sea is the beach.

I also love lighthouses. It's very exciting to see a lighthouse at night, with its great big light sweeping through the darkness. It would be fun to live in a lighthouse. Imagine having a round bedroom!

## Andrew McLean

Here I am in my studio. Luckily I have just cleaned up, or else it would look *really* messy. My dog's name is Kipper. We found him at the Lost Dogs Home. We don't know how he got the kink in his tail.

When I was growing up my dog was a black cocker spaniel called Donny. He could be clever sometimes. He would call out "Androo-oo-oo" when my mother called me for dinner, and he could climb ladders.

I think I would have liked to live in a lighthouse with Donny.